OPERATION REDUX

Written by
CAROLYN MILLER and BLAKE LEIBEL

Layouts by
TREVOR GORING

Illustrated by
JOSH ADAMS

Lettered and Designed by
DERON BENNETT
for AndWorld Design

Consulting Editor
CHRIS ROBINSON

Special Thanks to
STEPHEN CHRISTY

Executive Editors
JACK LATNER
GENEVA WASSERMAN

"Thanks to Chris, Stephen, Blake, Jack, Saori, Jane, Frenden and anybody else who had to put up with me over the course of doing this book. You've all proven you have the patience of Saints." - Josh

FANTASY PRONE, LLC
Blake Leibel, CEO
Jack Latner, President
Lawrence Longo, COO

WV ENTERPRISES
Wilmer Valderrama, CEO
Geneva Wasserman, President
Jeremy Ross, COO

Counsel:
Jeremy Tenser and Sean Marks

ISBN: 978-0-9903105-0-1

Published by FANTASY PRONE
in association with WV ENTERPRISES
c/o Pacific Design Center
8687 Melrose Ave., G271
West Hollywood, CA 90069
www.fantasyprone.com

OPERATION: REDUX. Original Graphic Novel, July 2014. OPERATION: REDUX TM and © 2014 Blake Leibel. FANTASY PRONE mark and logo, OPERATION: REDUX mark and logo, characters, and elements are trademarks of Blake Leibel. All Rights Reserved. No unauthorized reproductions permitted, except for review purposes. Any similarity to persons alive or dead is purely coincidental.

Printed in Korea

TOP SECRET

THIS IS A COVER SHEET

FOR CLASSIFIED INFORMATION

ALL INDIVIDUALS HANDLING THIS INFORMATION ARE REQUIRED TO PROTECT IT FROM UNAUTHORIZED DISCLOSURE IN THE INTEREST OF THE NATIONAL SECURITY OF THE UNITED STATES.

HANDLING, STORAGE, REPRODUCTION AND DISPOSITION OF THE ATTACHED DOCUMENTS WILL BE IN ACCORDANCE WITH APPLICABLE EXECUTIVE ORDER(S), STATUTE(S) AND AGENCY IMPLEMENTING REGULATIONS.

(This cover sheet is unclassified.)

TOP SECRET

703-101
NSN 7540-01-213-7901

STANDARD FORM 703 (6-85)
Prescribed by GSA/ISoo
32 cpr 2014

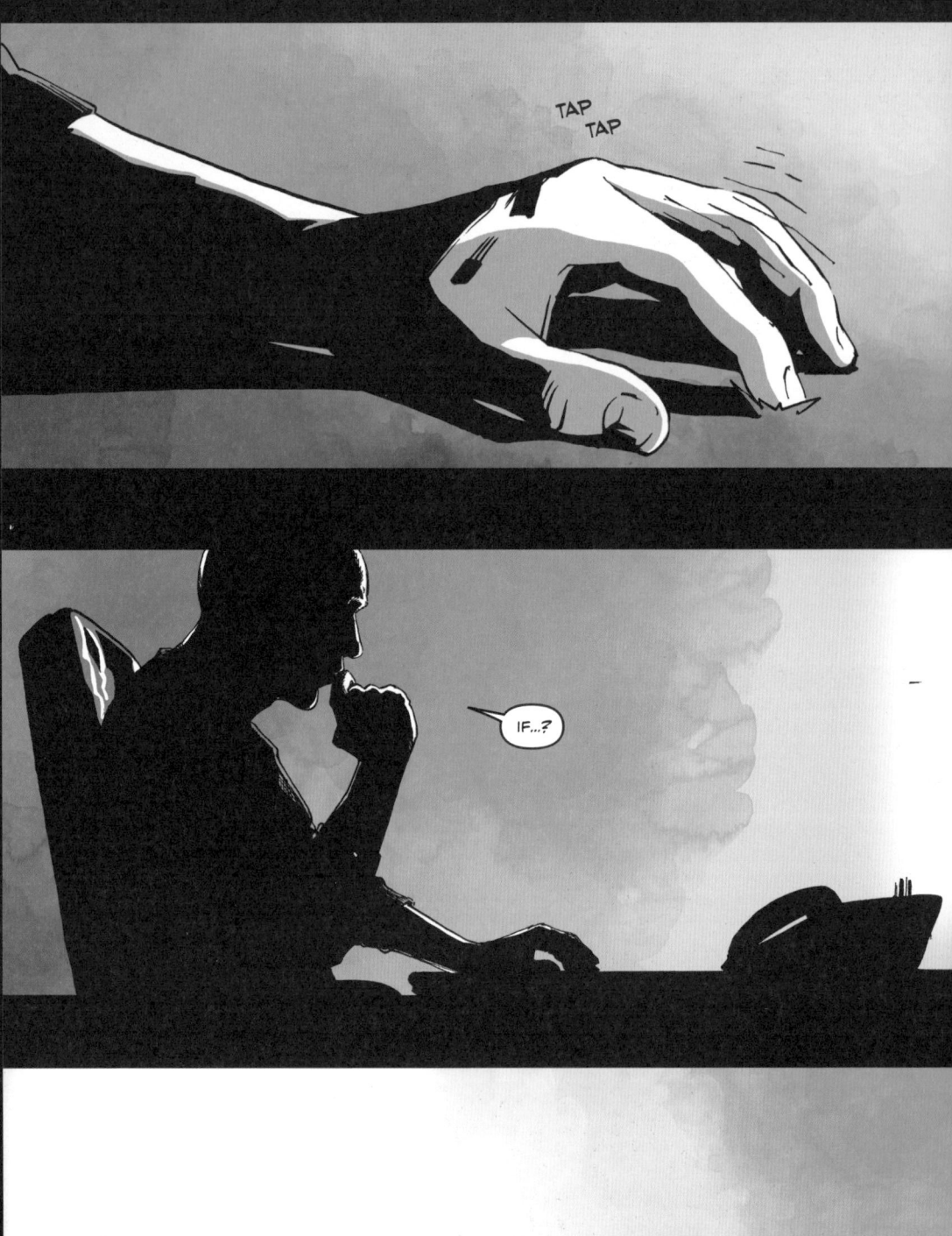

CHINO STATE PRISON

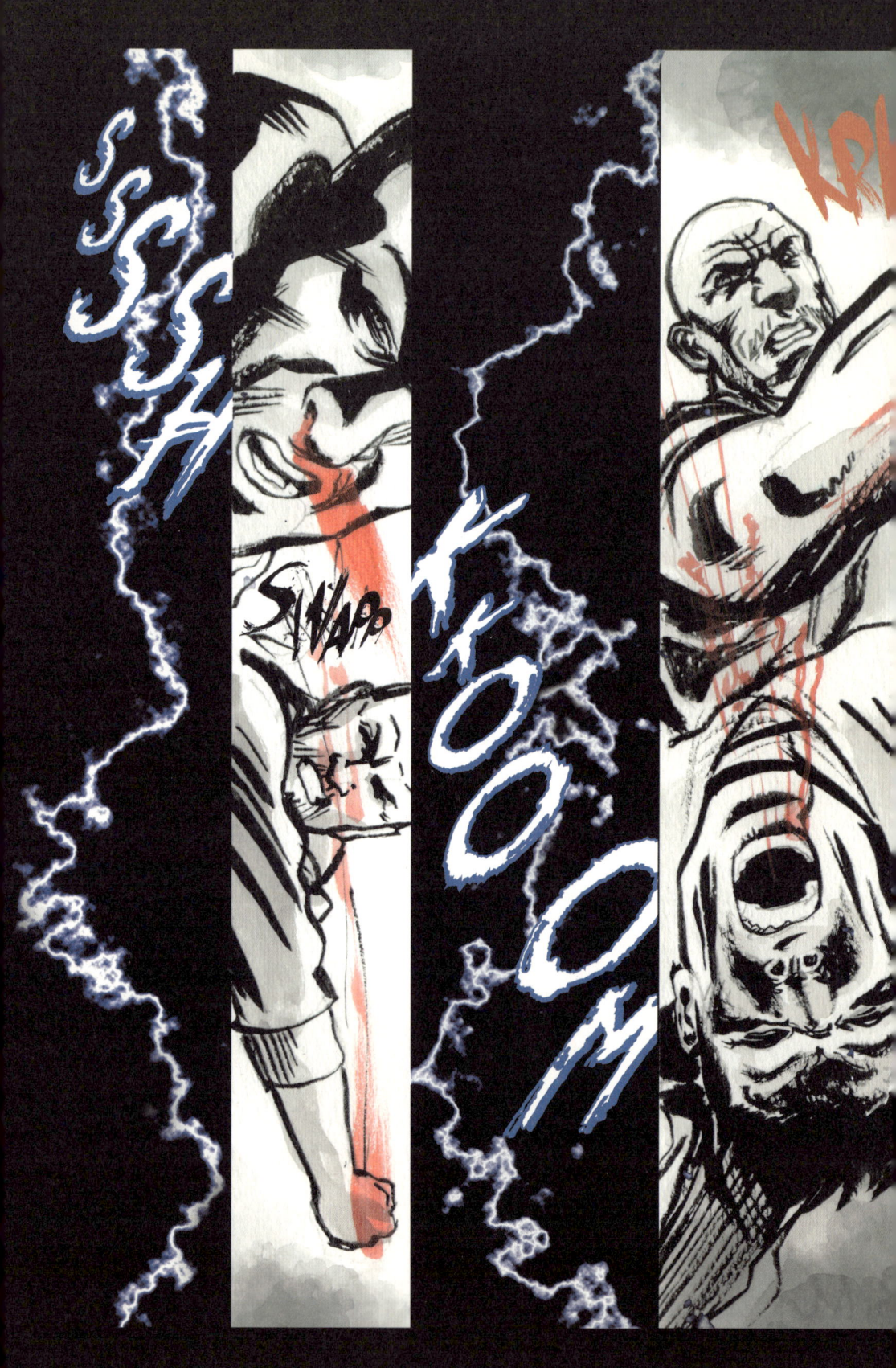

THE CITADEL · ISA HEADQUARTERS · VIRGINIA

I WANT TO GIVE HIM THE EXAM.

HIM?

HIM.

RURAL ARKANSAS

NINE YEARS LATER

DID WE TRACE THE STRAIN?

FROM A TEST TUBE OUT OF A LAB IN EGYPT.

THE TITLE FOR THE PROPERTY THEY WERE ALL LIVING ON IS TIED TO AN OFFSHORE COMPANY OWNED BY--

FELIX CLUSS.

THE FROZEN FOOD MAGNATE.

CLUSS IS A GERMAN-AMERICAN BILLIONAIRE WITH TIES TO THE NEO-NAZI MOVEMENT.

WHY WOULD THEY WORK TOGETHER?

I'M SORRY, REED... IT DOESN'T MAKE SENSE.

VENICE BEACH, CA

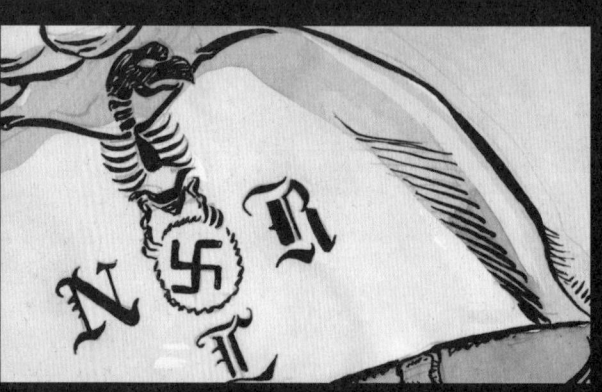

SHAMROCK SAM'S TATTOO PARLOR

CLUSS MANSION

PRIVATE ARMORY

FOREST LAWN CEMETARY

LAS VEGAS: ONE OF THREE ATMS IN THE COUNTRY THAT DISPENSES GOLD COINS.

CHANNEL 7 NEWS

...ON THE SCENE OF THE BRUTAL SLAYING OF LOCAL SCHOLARSHIP STUDENT, ERIN LASKEY...

...WHO WAS HUNG FROM THIS BRIDGE ALONG THE LA RIVER.

PENTHOUSE OFFICE. MILLENNIUM TOWERS.

I'M WATCHING NOW.

NO WITNESSES HAVE COME FORWARD. THE ONLY CLUE TO HIS DEATH-- THE SWASTIKA CARVED INTO HIS STOMACH.

IN RECENT MONTHS, MR. LASKEY BECAME LINKED TO A NEO-NAZI GROUP WHO DESIGNS RACIST VIDEO GAMES. HIS DEATH IS SUSPECTED TO BE RETALIATION FOR THE ESCALATING RACIAL TENSIONS BETWEEN GANGS IN THE LOS ANGELES AREA.

BUZZ COFFEE SHOP.

777 TOWER

FLUTE LESSON. THREE O'CLOCK. CECIL HOTEL. ROOM 421.

CHALET EDELWISS

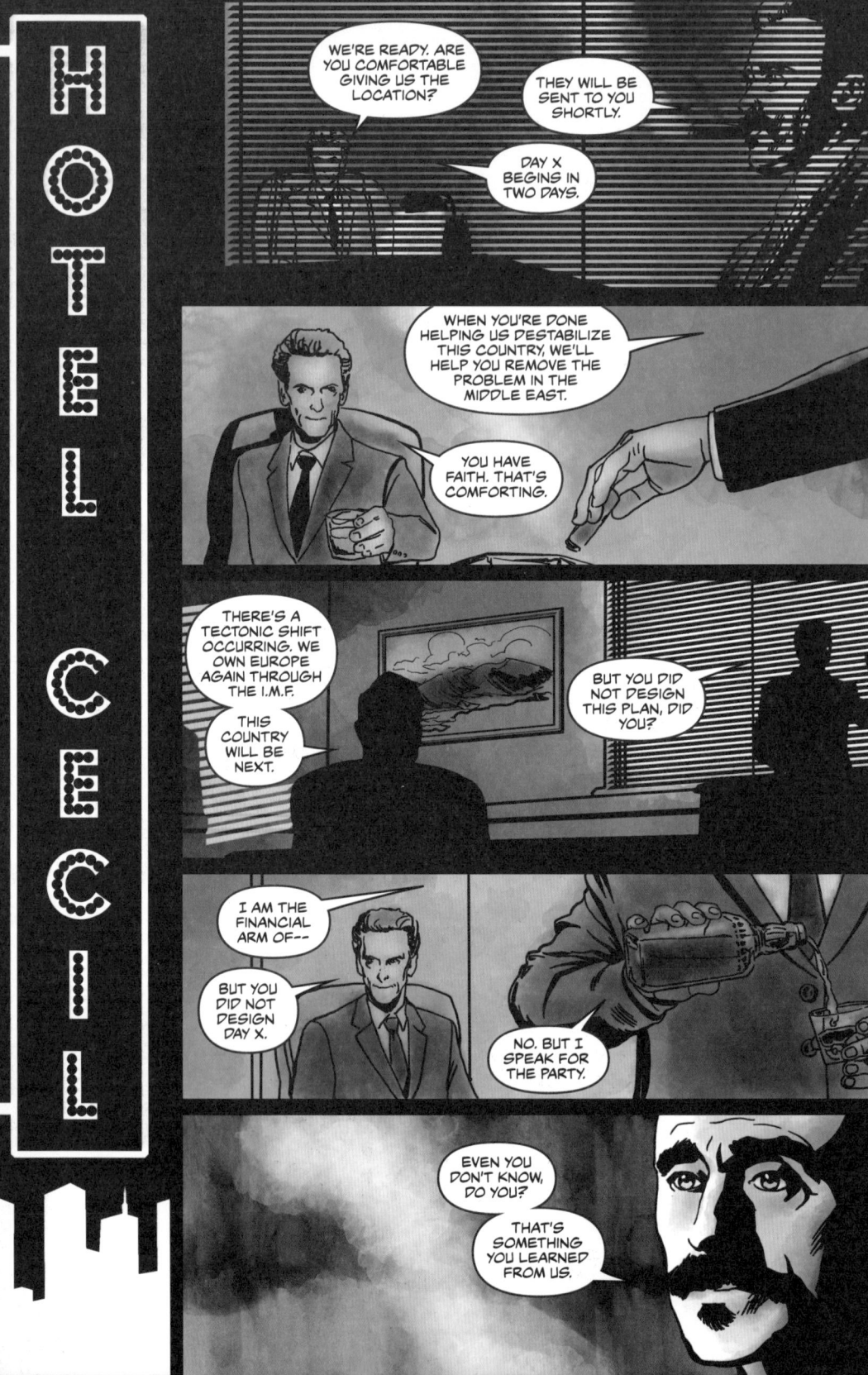

CLUSS MANSION

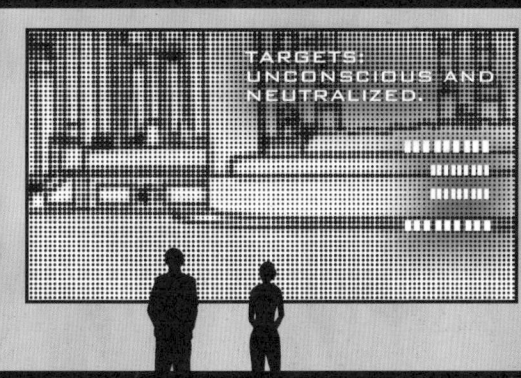

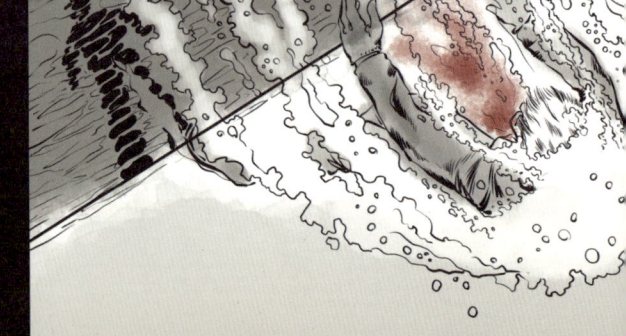

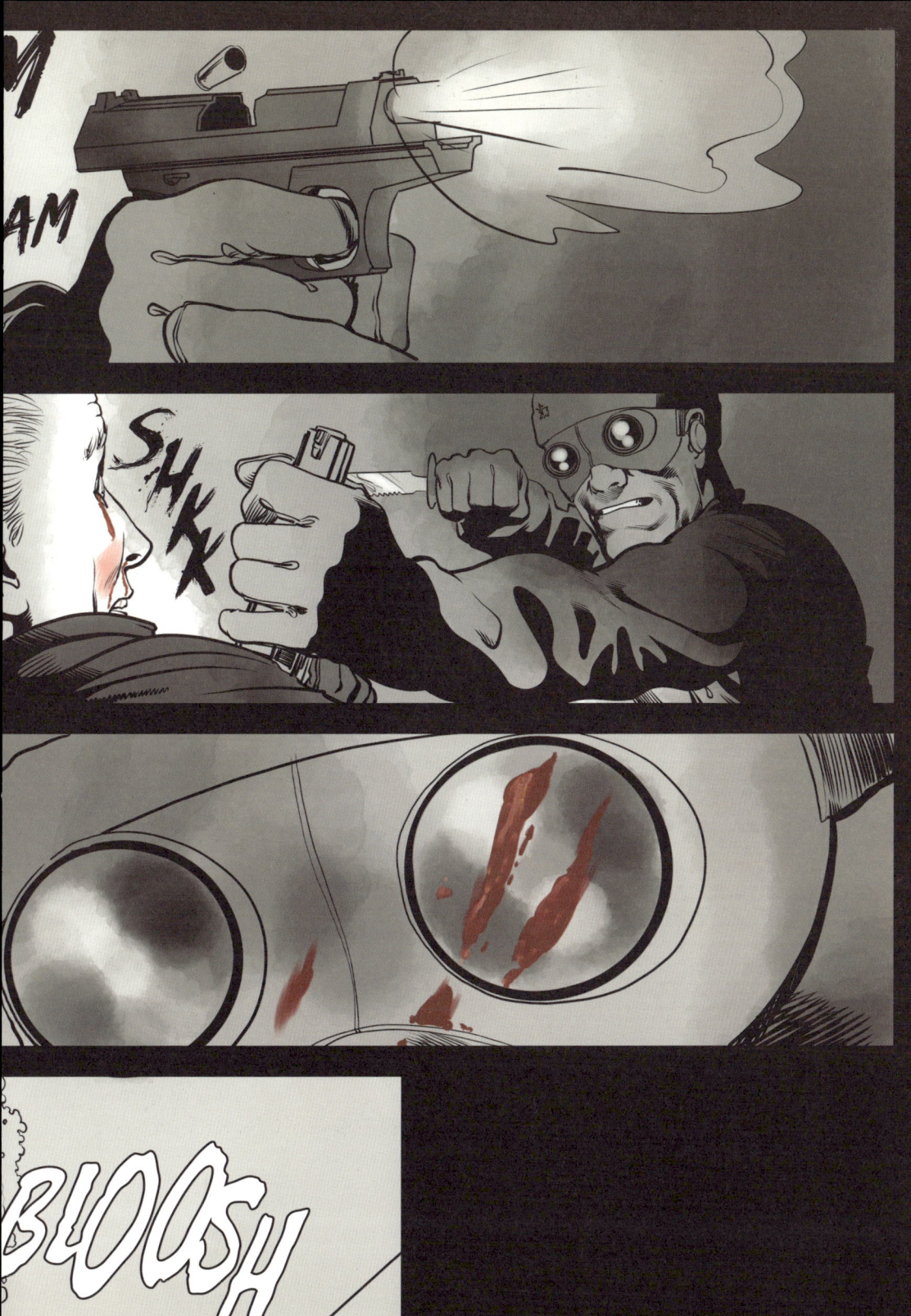

SAFE HOUSE · SKID ROW

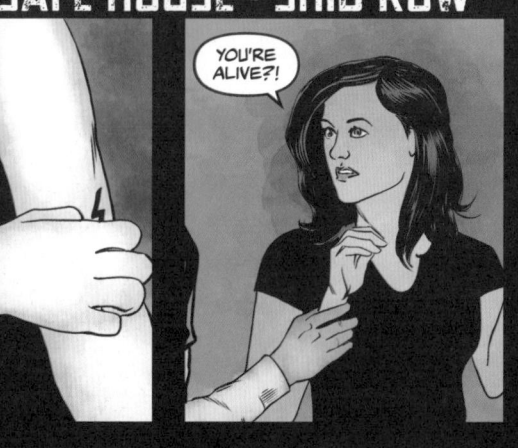

"YOU'RE ALIVE?!"

"BUT I HAVE NOTHING, CASSIE. TENS OF THOUSANDS WILL DIE."

"IF YOU KNOW SOMETHING, TELL ME. YOU'RE THE ONLY CHANCE I'VE GOT LEFT."

"HOW CAN I BE SURE I'LL BE SAFE."

"I'LL PROTECT YOU."

"YOU TRUST ME, JOSH?"

"YES."

"YOU CAME ALONE?"

PRIVATE AIRSTRIP

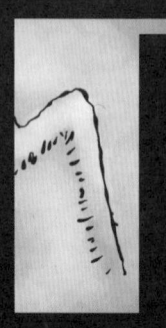

GREECE · GOLDEN DAWN HEADQUARTERS

BIOS

BLAKE LEIBEL is a director and writer who specializes in creating new worlds. He directs and writes for film and television in cartoon (*"Spaceballs: The Animated Series"*) and live action. He also created and wrote the comic book series *United Free Worlds* and created the acclaimed graphic novel *Syndrome* for Archaia. Before founding Fantasy Prone, Blake was the World Champion in the online video game Half-Life.

Born and raised in Los Angeles, **CAROLYN MILLER** has been fascinated by LA noir and thrillers as long as she can remember. As a filmmaker out of USC film school, she wrote and directed her first feature *UNDER STILL WATERS* as an homage to Roman Polanski. Professionally writing for film and television, when Blake Leibel invited her to collaborate on *OPERATION: REDUX* she jumped at the opportunity. This is her debut graphic novel.

JOSH ADAMS, trained by many of the industry's top talent, has racked up credits on titles such as *Doctor Who* (IDW Publishing), *House of Mystery* (DC Entertainment), *Batman Odyssey* (DC Entertainment), *Blood* (DarkHorse) as well as the *Astonishing X-Men Motion Comic* (Marvel) and countless hit projects for the Syfy Channel including *Battlestar Galactica, Stargate SG-1, Stargate Atlantis, Eureka, Ghost Hunters* and work for MTV and the WWE.

Eisner Award-nominated letterer **DERON BENNETT** has been providing lettering and production services for various comic book companies for the past decade. His body of work includes the critically acclaimed *Jim Henson's Tale of Sand, Jim Henson's The Dark Crystal, Mr. Murder is Dead, The Muppet Show Comic Book, Darkwing Duck,* and *Richie Rich*. He has recently published his first creator-owned comic book, *Quixote*.

(This page is classified.)

BIOS

STANDARD FORM 703 (6-85)
Prescribed by GSA/ISoo
32 cpr 2014

703-101
NSN 7540-01-213-7901